D1316765

Stella's Bull

Written by Frances Arrington   *Illustrated by* Aileen Arrington

Houghton Mifflin Company
Boston 1994

Library of Congress Cataloging-in-Publication Data

Arrington, Frances.
    Stella's bull / by Frances Arrington ; illustrated by Aileen
Arrington.
        p.   cm.
    Summary: Mary Wilson hears tales of a fearsome bull and blows the
stories up in her mind until she finally meets the bull face to
face.
    ISBN 0-395-67345-3
    [1. Bulls—Fiction. 2. Fear—Fiction.]   I. Arrington, Aileen,
ill. II. Title.
PZ7.A74337St 1994   93-29068
[E]—dc20   CIP
                            AC

Printed in the United States of America

BVG 10 9 8 7 6 5 4 3 2 1

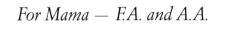

For Mama — F.A. and A.A.

MARY WILSON had never seen Stella's bull. She had never even seen Stella.

Stella's bull lived in the woods and fields past Black Creek on the way to town. He didn't like the sun. That's why you never saw him. He stayed in the shade of the trees. Willa Lee said so.

Willa Lee lived down the road in a small house where the bull had come one night, casting a shadow on her curtains and breathing outside her window.

Whenever the rain beat hard on the roof at night, Mary Wilson thought about Stella's bull thundering down the roads looking for something to kick. Whenever she saw a broken fence, she figured Stella's bull had been there.

Mary Wilson never set one foot on the property where Stella lived. With her bull.

Stella's bull was crazy.

One morning Mary Wilson was outside looking for her cat. She heard voices.

"Mary Wilson."

It's those Fitzpatricks, she thought.

The Fitzpatricks were on their way to Black Creek. They asked Mary Wilson if she was going. Mary Wilson said she was *not*.

"Don't y'all know Black Creek's over by Stella's?"

The Fitzpatricks didn't look one bit worried.

"Don't y'all know Stella's bull can smell creek water? Don't y'all know he could find his way there? Maybe he'll go for a swim the same way bird dogs do."

The Fitzpatricks just squinted in the morning sun, and one of them slapped at a gnat.

"If there's one thing I know'd make a bull mad, it'd be a pile of hollering children," Mary Wilson added. Fitzpatricks especially, only she left that part off. "So no thank you."

"That's dumb," said a Fitzpatrick.

"Well, it's true, so just go on," Mary Wilson said. She squinted at them and went back to calling the cat.

"What about Wade and Baby Rachel? They comin'?"

Mary Wilson sighed. She couldn't let her brother and sister go off to Black Creek. Stella's bull might get them.

"Got redbugs. Can't go," announced Mary Wilson, knowing very well redbugs had nothing to do with swimming. But it sounded good and she thought it would suit the Fitzpatricks. It did.

"Too bad," said still another Fitzpatrick, and they left, some of them beginning to scratch.

Mary Wilson found Willa Lee, and they went for a walk down Black Creek Road.

"Mary Wilson."

They looked up. The Fitzpatricks stood in the road grinning, their hair still wet with creek water.

"Weren't no bull at the creek," said one. "You made it up."

"Did not."

"Did."

"Willa Lee's *seen* the bull," Mary Wilson told them.

The Fitzpatricks looked at Willa Lee. Willa Lee said she'd seen the bull late one stormy night while crossing the train trestle. She said he was foaming at the mouth.

The Fitzpatricks looked at each other. They suddenly remembered they had somewhere to go.

September came and with it school. The only good thing about school was the first day. Mary Wilson decided to take all her new books home, the first day being the only day of the year she had a genuine interest in them.

It was a hot day and a heavy load, so Mary Wilson decided to get someone to carry her books. "It'll strengthen your pitching arm," she told Addison Fitzpatrick, and he believed her.

Just after the first creek bridge Addison started throwing the books back to Mary Wilson to check the strength of his arm. It was real strong.

All the books but one came straight to Mary Wilson. The spelling book cleared her head by three feet.

The book twirled on and on until it tumbled to the ground behind a barbed wire fence. Stella's barbed wire fence. And there it lay.

Mary Wilson looked at the book. It was near the woods in what looked like hoofprints.

Mary Wilson could run fast, but she couldn't get through a barbed wire fence fast. Bulls could run fast too, and bulls had horns, and Stella's bull was crazy.

Mary Wilson went home.

The following day Mary Wilson went to school with all her new books—all except the one lying in the dirt. The dirt with the hoofprints. The dirt behind Stella's barbed wire fence.

Not long after the bell rang, Mrs. Beasley wrote the spelling assignment on the blackboard. Mary Wilson tried to look busy.

"Where is your spelling book, Mary Wilson?"

Silence.

"Where is your spelling book, Mary Wilson Montgomery?" Mrs. Beasley repeated, slower this time.

"I'm sorry, Mrs. Beasley, but it's over on Black Creek Road behind Stella's fence."

"Oh?" Mrs. Beasley was speaking slower than ever now. "And you couldn't go pick it up?"

"Oh no, ma'am. I couldn't do that."

Silence.

Heads began to turn. This was going to be exciting.

She must be waiting for me to say something else, thought Mary Wilson. "Stella's bull's in there."

"Couldn't you go back when the bull isn't there and get it?"

"I've never seen Stella's bull," said Mary Wilson.

Mrs. Beasley pointed in the direction of the corner.

This was some way to start the fourth grade, thought Mary Wilson from her new place at the back of the room. She stuck out her tongue at Addison Fitzpatrick, but he wasn't looking. She wondered if Stella's bull had found her book and was at this very minute stomping a hole in it. And she decided that it was all Addison Fitzpatrick's fault.

Mary Wilson sat alone after school using the teacher's spelling book.

"I hope you will have your own book tomorrow," said Mrs. Beasley.

"Yes ma'am," said Mary Wilson.

After supper the book was still in Stella's field, and Mary Wilson was in left field, arms folded, chewing a wad of gum. Lila Beth was at bat, whining over a fair pitch. The only way Lila Beth's foot would ever touch a base was to be walked and Lila Beth knew it. This would take a while.

At first Mary Wilson didn't notice the sound in the woods behind her. But after a few minutes the rustling grew louder. Mary Wilson looked over her shoulder.

"It's Stella's bull!" she yelled.

Mary Wilson ran toward the schoolhouse. Half the field ran after her. The baseball and bat lay forgotten in the sand.

The flower trellis hit the ground before Mary Wilson had climbed it halfway to the schoolhouse roof.

"It's only a cow," someone said.

Mary Wilson got to her feet, rubbing her knees and elbows.

"Bet they heard you clear 'cross the county line."

Mary Wilson dusted off the palms of her hands.

"You know what Mary Wilson's middle name is?" said Addison Fitzpatrick. "Chicken Little. Mary Wilson Chicken Little Montgomery."

The next day Mary Wilson had made up her mind. She stayed after school to copy out of the teacher's spelling book, then started home. Only she wasn't really on her way home—she was on her way to Stella's field. And she wasn't going back to school again either. Not unless she had her spelling book—or she had really seen Stella's bull.

The road curved and she stopped at a broken fence. There'd been a storm the night before. Maybe Stella's bull had gotten out and been here. Mary Wilson searched the mud for hoofprints. If there'd been any, the rain had washed them away. She looked toward the woods for the bull, and then went on with the ground search.

Eyes on the ground, Mary Wilson stopped at a puddle. Beside the puddle lay her spelling book. She picked it up. Maybe Stella had found it and put it there, or maybe Stella's bull had kicked it over the fence. Mary Wilson slapped some sand off the cover, and as the sand scattered into the puddle, Mary Wilson froze. Something big and dark was moving closer and closer.

Mary Wilson looked up to see Stella's bull not more than ten feet away. He was standing in the tall grass across the barbed wire fence.

Mary Wilson blinked once. She dropped the book and ran, landing in a ditch on the other side of the road.

A minute passed. Then another. Some dog was barking, and Mary Wilson heard a mule wagon rumble over the creek bridge past Willa Lee's house. Mary Wilson stood up and stared. A horsefly buzzed past, and the bull's ears flicked. Mary Wilson just stood there.

It was Stella's bull all right. Funny thing, though. He wasn't tearing down fences. He was standing there minding his own business.

The wind blew the grass, and the bull stopped grazing to look at Mary Wilson.

"I know you," Mary Wilson whispered. "You're Stella's bull."

Mary Wilson went up the road and turned and stood watching Stella's bull move toward the line of trees.

She thought about what all she'd tell everyone and how she'd remember Stella's bull even when she grew up.

If she could have, Mary Wilson would have stayed longer. But the wind picked up and the rain came, and she had to go.

" 'Bye bull," whispered Mary Wilson.

And Stella's bull disappeared into the shelter of the trees.